LITTLE MISS LUCKY
IS GETTING MARRIED

Roger Hargreaves

Original concept and illustrations by
Roger Hargreaves

Written by
Sarah Daykin, Lizzie Daykin and Liz Bankes

EGMONT

This is Little Miss Lucky.

Little Miss Lucky just got engaged!

She's also just seen how much weddings cost …

'It's fine,' she said, 'I'll just do something simple with
a few friends and no fuss.'

'I completely agree,' said her mother. 'It's your day and
I won't interfere. I'll just leave this little book of ideas,
instructions and fabric samples here …'

'… and drop the other four volumes round later.'

MR. MEN   LITTLE MISS

MR. MEN™ LITTLE MISS™ © THOIP (a SANRIO company)

Little Miss Lucky is Getting Married © 2018 THOIP (a SANRIO company)
Printed and published under license from Penguin Random House LLC
Published in Great Britain by Egmont UK Limited
2 Minster Court, 10th Floor, London EC3R 7BB

ISBN 978 1 4052 9222 1
69054/005
Printed in Italy

Little Miss Lucky's bridesmaids couldn't wait to get involved.

'I've got you a colour-coded folder for your wedmin,' said Little Miss Wise, her sensible friend from primary school.

'I've got you a stripper for the hen do!' said Little Miss Naughty, her crazy friend from uni. 'And I've ordered devil horns, L-plates and straws shaped like–'

'WELLIES!' said Little Miss Wise. 'We'll need wellies if we're going glamping.'

'Brilliant,' said Little Miss Lucky. 'Just as long as we keep it simple!'

But the big day was already getting bigger …

… and so was her mum's wedding hat.

'Now, for the table decorations I'm thinking lilac napkins to complement the prawn vol-au-vents – five hundred should be enough, but you know what Mr Greedy's like around a buffet. What did we decide on the ice sculptures – dolphins, parrots or beavers? Aunt Dotty wants to know if there's a free bar, Cousin Fussy wants to know where he's sitting and Uncle Clumsy's asked if you can pick him up from the station on the way to the church?'

Little Miss Lucky reached for the gin.

The hen do preparations were in full swing.

LITTLE MISS WISE
Hey hens! So we're thinking cottage in the Cotswolds, vintage cream tea and bonnet-making.

LITTLE MISS NAUGHTY
And loads of booze!

LITTLE MISS WISE
So if everyone could send over their favourite memory of Little Miss Lucky and a £500 deposit by Friday, that would be great. :) Xxxxxx

LITTLE MISS WISE
P.S. Don't worry – I'll take care of the food this time!

(They didn't want a repeat of Little Miss Brainy's hen do when the hog roast was somewhat undercooked.)

Meanwhile, Little Miss Lucky was regretting handwriting the invitations and briefly considered stabbing out her own eyes with the calligraphy pen.

She went to find her fiancé to see if he wanted to elope, but was confused to find him wearing a foil cape and playing with his lightsaber.

'How would you feel about a sci-fi theme?' he said. 'I thought maybe you could dress up as a sexy alien and we could do our vows in Klingon.'

Little Miss Lucky didn't think it could get any worse, until she was bound, gagged and thrown in the back of a bus.

'Surprise! It's HEN DO time!' shouted Little Miss Naughty.

'On it till we vomit!' whooped Little Miss Whoops.

'Great,' said the groom's cousin, who they hadn't expected to turn up and whose name they couldn't remember.

And so the hen do began, with a five-hour traffic jam, where Little Miss Wise handed out their first task – making self-portraits with dried bits of pasta. Meanwhile Little Miss Naughty cracked open her third bottle of prosecco and played 'I Have Never' with Little Miss Lucky's mum.

The next morning, Little Miss Wise handed out the day's itinerary, with 'helpful' suggestions from Little Miss Naughty.

9:00 Karaoke breakfast   <--- SHOTS

9:35 Glitter paintballing   <--- MORE SHOTS

10:00 Watch chick flicks, pillow fight, plait each other's hair

11:00 Life drawing <---- YES PLEASE!

11:30 Snake charming

12:00 Indoor white water rafting

12:30 ~~Picnic~~ LIQUID lunch

13:30 Spoken word (bring your rap)   <--- EVEN MORE SHOTS

14:00 Act out bride's most embarrassing moments

14:30 Go to Micropig Café

14:45 Take cute Instagram pics with micropigs

15:00 Sausage making

(Page 1 of 19)

Everything was running to schedule, but unfortunately there hadn't been time for Little Miss Naughty's suggestions.

'Has everyone finished their naked man drawing?' said Little Miss Wise. 'I'll be marking them soon.'

'Sorry Miss, my micropig ate mine,' said Little Miss Trouble.

The hens were enjoying the activities, but they did think Little Miss Wise was being a bit strict.

Little Miss Chatterbox didn't appreciate having her phone confiscated during bonnet-making.

And Little Miss Stubborn wasn't best pleased about having to sit out of pole-dancing after forgetting her nipple tassels.

'Is it time to go to the pub?' asked Little Miss Curious.

'Actually, our next activity is decorating knickers,' said Little Miss Wise.

'Did someone say pub?' said Little Miss Naughty, already distributing phallic straws, pulling on her 'Let's Get Lucky' T-shirt and painting big red Ls everywhere.

'HOORAY!' cried the hens, grabbing some loo roll and fashioning Little Miss Lucky a makeshift wedding dress.

And so the hens were ready to fly the nest, spread their feather boa wings and get totally wasted.

Little Miss Lucky was just being shuffled into a taxi when she noticed that someone was missing …

She eventually found Little Miss Wise huddled in the corner crying into a pile of knickers.

'I just wanted everyone to have fun!' she sobbed.

'They are!' said Little Miss Lucky.

'And for you to have the perfect hen do!'

'I am!' said Little Miss Lucky.

'And for you to have hundreds of pairs of knickers embroidered with our favourite memories of you!'

Little Miss Lucky didn't know what to say.

Eventually she had an idea. They could bring the knickers with them and finish the activities in the pub!

'Yes! We could do a pub scavenger hunt!' said Little Miss Wise excitedly. 'I'll put it on the itinerary!'

It was a night to remember … though few of them did after Little Miss Curious made them sample every drink on the menu. Little Miss Chatterbox chatted up all the Mr Men in sight, Little Miss Whoops lost her shoes and her dignity in a dance battle and Little Miss Tidy was sick in a bin.

The groom's cousin was about to start her rap titled 'My name is …' when Little Miss Lucky's mum got them chucked out of the club for grinding at the bar.

But up the road, a gleaming light beckoned them to the place where every great night should end. The kebab shop.

'Screw the wedding diet!' said Little Miss Lucky, diving head first into her cheesy chips.

The sleeping hens were rudely awoken by the sound of screaming. Little Miss Wise had just caught sight of herself in the mirror. They crawled slowly out of bed, vowing never to drink again.

A rather wobbly Little Miss Whoops was in charge of the hangover breakfast, but fifty smashed eggs later they resorted to eating their pasta self-portraits.

'I've had the best hen do ever,' said Little Miss Lucky, face down on the floor. Her phone beeped – apparently the last anyone had seen of the groom he was tied to a lamp post in Stag Do Land.

Suddenly they noticed the state of the cottage. The place was covered in glitter, wine stains and now eggs!

Luckily Little Miss Naughty had booked a butler-in-the-buff who was rather handy with a feather duster and who arrived just in time to clean the whole house.

In fact, Little Miss Lucky's mum was so impressed that she asked if he'd give her downstairs a once over.

'What's next on the itinerary?' asked Little Miss Lucky.

'Let me have a look,' said Little Miss Wise.

'Oh … it looks like you're getting married!'

'WHAT!?' screeched Little Miss Lucky. 'WE SLEPT FOR A WHOLE DAY!!'

But, luckily for Little Miss Lucky, she had her hens.

'We can make you another loo roll wedding dress!' said Little Miss Naughty.

'You can wear these devil horns as a tiara!' said her mum.

'I've brought everything you need for the wedding with us,' said Little Miss Wise. 'To the hen do bus everyone! We've still got to pick up Uncle Clumsy on the way.'

Thankfully Little Miss Lucky made it to the spaceship marquee on time. And so did the groom, once they'd wired him an emergency passport.

And even though the ring-bearing doves pooed on the congregation, Aunt Dotty lost her teeth in the chocolate fountain, and the best man's speech made them cry for all the wrong reasons, everyone still had a great time.

Little Miss Lucky looked around at them all – her mum in her massive hat, the hens, still coated in glitter, and her husband, dressed as a sexy alien.

She felt like the luckiest Little Miss in the world.

The only thing left was to throw the bouquet and see who would be getting married next …

… 'Caught it!' yelled her mum, giving the butler-in-the-buff a cheeky wink.